PATRICK

Adventures in
Early Little League

DAVID METZGER, AUTHOR

Robert Fowler, Illustrator

ISBN: 978-1-09837-111-1

Any references to historical events, real people, or real places are used fictitiously. Other names, characters, and places are products of the author's imagination.

FOREWORD

Patrick is a ten-year-old living in in Williamsport, Pennsylvania, the city where Little League began. He diligently throws baseballs at a target he chalked on a concrete wall to prepare for the coming Little League season. He has a strong arm and a good aim. His adventures put him in constant touch with grown-ups. He looks them in the eye when he talks to them. A famous ball player provides him some pitching tips, and he eagerly accepts the advice. His throwing not only comes in handy dealing with a bully, but also wins him the starting pitcher position in the regular Little League season. His pitching skills draw criticisms from the dads of the batters he continually strikes out. This leads to a meeting with the Little League Board. At the end of the regular season, the first National Little League Tournament, (later called the Little League World Series), is scheduled to start. As a successful pitcher in the regular season, Patrick fully expects to be picked for the team that will represent his league in the first Little League National Tournament. His regular season coach comes to his house with the news. The ups and downs in Patrick's life from then on are a roller coaster ride, the best of days and the worst of days. Whether up or down, Patrick approaches life with honesty, courage, team loyalty, and quick wits. Life for him is an unrelenting adventure.

About the Author

David Metzger, a writer, lives in Virginia with his wife, Christine. His published works include articles written and lectures given while a practicing lawyer, a business book: "While the Nation Slept: The Struggles of Innovative Small Businesses in the U.S., and the Patrick Trilogy, a series of three historical fiction works for young readers: "Patrick: The Adventures of an Early American Boy," "Patrick: Adventures Along the Oregon Trail," and "Patrick: Adventures in Early Little League."

This book is the third in a series about fictional ten-year-old boys named Patrick. The first book is set in America's pre-Revolutionary War era. The second describes adventures of a 19th century Patrick along the Oregon Trail. This third fictional tale is set in post-World War II America, and involves the early days of Little League. These books strive to entertain, and also to educate the young reader.

About the Illustrator

Robert Fowler, a self-taught painter and illustrator, lives in Michigan, with his wife, Rona. He has sold many paintings, many of western U.S. scenes of cowboys and the American West. He has illustrated the entire Patrick Trilogy, and other children's works. Fowler has received numerous awards for his art, including a "Best in Show" first place finish at a Wyoming State Fair and a "Best in Show" first place finish at an Arizona Yavapai County Fair. Several major collections include his art.

ACKNOWLEDGEMENTS

I thank my son, Jonathan, for inspiring this work. When informed that I wanted to write a different book, Jonathan asked: "Why don't you write one about Patrick?" I used to tell youthful Jonathan "Patrick" bed-time stories. Fictional Patrick was a stone-thrower in those early stories. Hopefully, those bed-time stories, in a small way, inspired Jonathan's journey as a baseball star at Little League, Babe Ruth League, high school, Show Case, college, and professional levels.

I also acknowledge and thank Robert Fowler for his artistic contributions to this work. As one can see from the preceding "About the Illustrator" segment, Mr. Fowler is an accomplished, self-taught artist, and has illustrated other young readers' books. He patiently balanced the constraints of historical representation, text, and my vision in each of the three books in this series.

Many thanks go to Dany Turner of Next Generation Designs, of Westlake, Virginia, and to Robbie Downey of Print-n-Paper, of Westlake, Virginia, for their excellent contributions in laying out the book. Thanks also go to the terrific team at BookBaby—Ramona Pina, Publishing Specialist, and Amanda VanMeter, Distribution—for their publishing support.

I also owe thanks to my patient wife, who supported my journey in writing and publishing this trilogy.

I dedicate this book to our son, Jonathan. As a youth, his athletic activities included soccer, swimming, gymnastics, basketball, and baseball. As he progressed, circumstances forced him to make choices, and he concentrated on swimming and baseball. Worried about making the high school baseball team, he hit against a pitching machine until his hands bled. I caught his practice pitches until their speed made it dangerous to do so. He made the team as both a pitcher and hitter. As a senior, he pitched his team into the Commonwealth of Virginia's Final Championship game, and during that year, set a record for doubles. His senior high school relay swim team came within .01 of a second of an All-American record. Our home has an extensive display of his swimming medals and trophies, among many others, all won as he fought chronic asthma. The University of Virginia drafted him to play baseball, where he pitched for three years. The Kansas City Royals drafted him at the end of his junior year (He graduated later.).He threw 93 miles per hour from the left side in college, and as a professional. In the face of arm and shoulder surgeries at the professional level, he displayed a grit and determination to come back and play. Each rehabilitation recovery involved hard, lonely, grueling work. He displayed that same grit and determination to succeed in business after baseball. In every endeavor, he gives it his all. He married Rebecca, and they have given us two grandsons, Lincoln and Beckett. As a Christian, son, husband, father, businessman, and competitor, we are, as my mother would have allowed us to say of Jonathan: "humbly proud" of him.

David Metzger, Author

CHAPTER 1

Ten-year-old Patrick felt like he was running for his life. Gregory, an older and bigger boy, was chasing him. Again. Gregory had never caught him, and Patrick wasn't going to let that happen this time.

Patrick ran down one street and up another. He turned, and entered a wide parking lot hosting a farmer's market. The farmers' tables, filled with fruits and vegetables, gave him a plan. As he passed a table of vegetables, he grabbed two hard tomatoes.

Patrick turned and faced the bully. Gregory stopped in his tracks. No younger boy he chased had ever confronted him before. Patrick took a stance, turned his body, took a step and fired a tomato—turned laser—into Gregory's stomach. The bully was speechless. He hurt in two places—his stomach and his ego. As he started toward Patrick, a second missile hit him in the chest.

"Ouch, you bully!" he shouted at Patrick.

Patrick thought to himself, "Coward," and walked away. His bravery in confronting his nemesis had paid off.

Patrick walked home, picked out two baseballs he kept in his room, and walked to what he called the "Wall." Someone had painted this concrete wall green. Near the tennis courts, tennis players practiced hitting serves and shots against it. Patrick used it for something else.

On it, he had drawn a rectangle target with white chalk. The bottom of it came to his knees, the top below his shoulders. It was just under a foot and a half wide. He dropped one ball and took his stance. Right-handed, he turned his left shoulder to the target, and extended his left arm toward the target. The rectangle appeared just above his glove. He turned his body, and took a step forward. His right arm followed through like a catapult, and he hit the target. He threw again, just missing it. Upset with himself, he tried again, taking more time to sight the target above his glove. Success.

After fifty balls, he inspected the baseball. The seams were coming apart and it had a flat spot. He trashed it on the way home. Replacement baseballs consumed most of his earnings.

When he entered the house through the back door, he sensed something was wrong. His mother was sitting at the kitchen table. Across from her was a man who seemed vaguely familiar.

"Patrick," his mother said sternly. "Did you steal tomatoes from this farmer?"

Patrick knew he was in trouble. He could tell by her expression that she hoped it wasn't true. But his mother constantly stressed how important it was to tell the truth.

"I took two of them," Patrick said, looking the man in the eye.

"I saw you take them," the man said. "A friend told me where you lived. I worked hard to grow those tomatoes. I saw how you used them, too."

"Patrick," his mother said. "Is there something you want to tell me?"

Patrick took a deep breath. He had never told his parents about Gregory. He said slowly: "Gregory chases me a lot. I'm afraid of him. I got sick of running from him. So when I passed the tomato stand, I grabbed two and threw them at him."

His mother was speechless. The man spoke: "Five cents per tomato will suffice."

"Patrick, go get ten cents from your bank," his mother said sternly, trying to get over the fact that her son never told her about the bully.

Patrick went to his room, coaxed a dime out of his treasure chest/piggy bank, and returned to the kitchen. He handed it to the man. This was no fun. He earned the money by growing things in his garden for Mom. He needed the dime for baseballs.

The man stood up and spoke. "That's honest of you. And I'm impressed that you paid it, not your mother. I'm not going to keep this." He handed the dime back to Patrick. He continued: "Gregory chases my son, too, while we're here, from the farm. He's afraid of Gregory. Maybe this will end the bullying." With that, the farmer got up and left.

"We need to talk," his mother said. Patrick told her about how Gregory had chased him around the neighborhood for months, taunting him, calling him names, and threatening to beat him. And how Patrick used his arm to end it. Mom gave him a hug.

"I'm proud of you," she said. "But you should have told me sooner."

Patrick returned the dime to his bank. He needed another baseball.

CHAPTER 2

The next day, Patrick was back at the Wall, practicing throwing, as he had done for the past year. The practice strengthened his arm. He recently started working on hitting parts of the rectangle, like the corners, or the upper, lower, inside, or outside halves. Then something happened that changed everything. A man standing behind him called out: "Hey kid!"

Patrick turned around and the man extended his hand. As they shook hands, the man said: "Hi, I'm Bob Feller. I was talking to Carl Crotz about support for his Little League. He said you might be here."

"Wow! Bob Feller! The pitcher?" Patrick asked. Patrick didn't know who this Carl Crotz guy was or why he would know Patrick, but he knew about Bob Feller and his famous fastball.

"Yes," Feller replied "Do you mind if I show you something?" "Sure," Patrick said. He was almost trembling with excitement. Feller showed Patrick how to hold his fastball differently than he usually did. The ball acted differently when he threw it.

"Did you see how it tailed off at the end? It will bend in on a right-handed hitter," Feller explained. "Let me show you something else," Feller said. Feller held the ball in his palm. When Patrick threw it that way, it was much slower than his fastball.

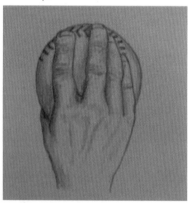

"There are two ways to throw a change-up. This palm ball is easier than a circle change. You don't have to twist your arm with it. This pitch is a big change in speed from your fastball. Get it near the strike zone, and you'll strike out batters with it."

"Thanks!" said Patrick, aware that it sounded a little too loud.

"Practice these pitches," Feller said, then turned and left. Patrick couldn't wait to tell his parents he had met Bob Feller.

***

After meeting Feller, Patrick practiced the palm ball. He called it the Change because of the difference in speed from his fastball. He was throwing it again today. Accuracy was a big problem with this pitch, but he kept practicing it with the other pitch Feller showed him.

He was also experimenting with another pitch. A tennis player gave him the idea. By turning his wrist, he put spin on it. It would curve down and away from a right-handed hitter. He called it the Curve.

There was a sense of urgency. Little League started in a few days. He especially wanted to get these pitches under control before the games started. He wanted to pitch. He had to be good enough.

Suddenly, he heard a voice behind him. "What are you doing?"

He turned. A girl about his age was watching him.

"Practicing my throwing," he replied. He was puzzled about why she cared about what he was doing.

"That last one was different than the others," she said.

"I call it my Change, he said. He couldn't think of anything else to say.

"My name is Wanda," the girl said. She sensed he was shy and struggling for words. "What's your name?" "Patrick," he replied.

"I'd like to hear about your pitching," she said. "Do you want to get an ice cream when you're finished?"

"Sure," Patrick said, impressed that she used the word "pitching." "But I need to throw five more." He was at forty-five throws.

He threw five more Changes and turned to Wanda. "Let's get that ice cream," he said.

As they walked, Wanda talked to him about his throwing. She asked a question that took him by surprise.

"Do you throw your Change in the same way you throw your other pitches?" Wanda asked.

"I try to, but it's hard," Patrick said.

"Well, wouldn't it help if you alternated throwing your fastball and the Change?" she asked. "Would that help you throw the Change the same way you throw your fastball?"

Her suggestion took Patrick by surprise. It made sense. Holding the Change in his palm took the speed off the pitch, but it was hard to control. A consistent arm motion would help.

"You might be right," Patrick said, turning to face her. "I never thought of that. Yes, it would help." He made a note to himself: "This girl is interested in baseball."

Wanda got Patrick talking about the upcoming Little League season on the way to the ice cream shop. He had a chocolate fudge, three-scoop cone. She had two scoops of strawberry, and listened to him talk the whole time. She was smiling, not just at him, but at the success she had in getting him to talk.

"Thanks for the suggestion," Patrick said, as they headed to their homes.

The next day he alternated throwing the Change with his

four-seam fastball. He tried to keep his arm motion consistent for both pitches. He tried holding the Change with his fingers a little straighter, but the ball still in his palm. The Change started hitting the target. He thought of Wanda. Before her, Feller was the only one who had ever commented on his throwing. Her advice was good enough to use.

He looked at his two baseballs. Both were tattered. He needed to work in his garden to earn money to buy new ones.

CHAPTER 3

Patrick was on the mound, facing his first batter. He had dreamed of this day. Ever since he had heard of this new sport called Little League, he had had wanted to play. And not just play. Pitch. His year-long throwing against the Wall led to this day.

His first practice had been one of the most exciting days of his young life, topped only by today. It took no time at all for Coach Kirby to identify his starting pitcher.

Patrick couldn't believe it when Coach Kirby said: "Patrick, you will be starting the first game." All of his teammates agreed that was the right decision.

Robby called for a fastball as the first pitch. Patrick wound, sighted the catcher's glove above the glove in his left hand, and let it fly. The batter let it go.

"Strike one!" the umpire cried. He was a dad of a player from the other team. But he was honest, because it was right down the middle.

Robby called for another fastball, and put his glove toward the inside of this right-handed batter. Patrick saw why. The batter was crowding the plate. Patrick put a fastball on the inside half of the plate. The batter backed away.

"Strike two!" the umpire dad yelled.

""Wow!" Patrick heard from in back of him. It came from the on-deck hitter.

The hitter backed away from the plate. Robby set up outside. Patrick pictured Robby's glove as the left half of his chalked rectangle. He hit his spot. The batter swung too late and missed.

"Strike three!" The next two batters grounded out.

Patrick's Red Sox scored three runs in their first time ever at the plate. Tommy, the shortstop, hit a lead-off double down the right field line. Jiménez, the center fielder, hit him in with a double down the left field line. The third batter, Charlie, the right fielder, hit a blooper over the second baseman's head that fell in for a hit. The fielder quickly picked it up and looked for the runner.

"Go Jimmy!" the Red Sox bench was screaming. When the ball landed, Jimmy had taken off. He rounded third like a house afire, never slowing down. He stormed into home plate with a slide, just ahead of the throw.

"Safe!" the umpire called. The Red Sox scored one more run that inning.

The next inning, the lead-off batter hit a first-pitch grounder to short. Tommy picked it up, and with a strong arm, easily threw out the runner. Patrick struck out the next two.

The Red Sox scored more runs that inning. With two men on, Patrick came to bat. The pitcher threw a ball outside. Patrick simply didn't swing at pitches that weren't over the plate.

Patrick took a hard swing at the next pitch and hit it right back to the pitcher. He dropped it, and the ball rolled out in front of him. From the stands, the pitcher's father yelled: "Got 'im!" The high school baseball coach, who was watching the game, and had attended Red Sox practices, turned and said to the father: "Not so fast."

The pitcher went to the ball, picked it up, turned to first base, wound up a little, and finally threw it. Too late. Fleet-footed Patrick had already stepped on the base. The umpire called Patrick safe. The high school coach turned around and smiled at the pitcher's father.

By the third inning, the batters were ready for Patrick's fastball. Robby came out to the mound. "OK," he said. "So they got two hits in a row. Give me that other fastball, then the curve."

Patrick held his fastball differently. It tailed in a little at the end, toward the right-handed batter, who let it go. The umpire called it a strike. If the movement on the fastball confused the batter, he was not ready for Patrick's Curve. It started on the same line as the fastball. The batter swung and missed as the ball curved away at the end. The swing was also ahead of this slower pitch.

It went like that for the rest of the game. When batters on the other team started telling each other to watch for the curveball, Robby started calling for the straight fastball again. The other team hit mostly weak infield grounders.

Unnoticed by Patrick or his teammates, a man with a clip board was taking notes on the sidelines. He wrote: "Hitting," on top of his paper. When Jimmy rounded third, he noted: "Base running." And because Coach Kirby at third had sent him home, he wrote: "Coaching." After Patrick struck out his eighth batter, he wrote: "Pitching." In the sixth inning, a batter connected with Patrick's straight fastball with a runner on first. The hit went deep into center field. Jiménez turned and started running toward it. He caught the ball on a dead run, spun around, and rifled a throw to second to double up the runner. As Patrick tipped his hat to Jimmy, the man noted: "Fielding."

The Red Sox won 13-4. As he was walking off the field, Patrick heard a high-pitched: "Woohoo!" behind him. He turned around. Wanda was standing on the third base line. She waved.

As team members slapped Patrick's back, Coach Kirby watched with concern as parents from the other team left, loudly complaining.

"This game is supposed to be about hitting," one said. Another loudly agreed. "It's the pitcher's job to put the ball down the middle so batters can hit it." A third agreed. "This pitching stuff is boring."

The first dad then said something that Coach Kirby caught: "We're going to the Board."

Coach said to himself: "That's trouble."

CHAPTER 4

Patrick was working in his garden hoeing green beans. He was getting rid of weeds and loosening up the soil so it would absorb water. It was early summer. He was living off last year's earnings. These bean plants represented future revenues. He would pick beans when ready. Mom gave him three cents for each quart she canned.

His mother called to him from the house: "Patrick, you have a visitor."

Coach Kirby greeted him in the kitchen. "Patrick, I am headed to the Little League Board. They're hearing some parents' complaints today."

"About what?" Patrick asked. He beat his mother to the question.

"Well," Coach Kirby said slowly, "about you. Some dads have complained that you strike out too many batters. They claim that's not the way the game should be played."

"Are they right?" Patrick's mother asked.

"No," the Coach replied. "Let me be clear. Patrick has done nothing wrong. They're upset that their sons can't hit Patrick's pitching."

The Coach went on: "Patrick, the Board invited you to attend, but you don't have to come. If you would prefer not to appear before this Board of grown-ups, I can do this alone."

"No, no," Patrick said. "I'm coming with you." Coach Kirby's challenge had the right effect on Patrick.

The coach said, "Let's go." To Patrick's concerned mother, he said: "He's going to be OK." Nonetheless, she came along.

The Board met at the local school. They sat at a long set of tables. Another table and chair faced them. When Coach Kirby and Patrick arrived, a Board member quickly placed a second chair at the table facing the Board. Before he sat down, Patrick noticed three men seated on chairs behind him. Mom sat down in back of them.

The man obviously in charge spoke: "Coach Kirby, thank you for coming." He then spoke to Patrick: "Patrick, I presume."

"Yes sir," Patrick replied respectfully. "I'm Patrick."

The man in charge spoke again: "My name is Carl Crotz. I'm the Chairman of this Board. With me are the Little League Board members: George and Bret Bebble, and their wives, Annabelle and Eloise, John and Peggy Lindemuth, and my wife, Grayce. We like to say that we started Little League here in Williamsport, and are helping it grow."

Crotz went on: "As you may know, this is the first year we will have a Little League series called the National Little League Tournament. We are pretty excited about that."

Coach Kirby and Patrick said nothing.

Crotz continued: "We convened today because some dads complained to the Board about the last Red Sox game. Their chief concern seems to be that Patrick mercilessly strikes out their sons."

Crotz looked at the dads from the other team. They were not amused by his making light of their concerns.

Crotz went on: "They claim that your job, Patrick, is to throw pitches down the middle of the plate—not too fast—so their sons can hit them. They claim that Little League is, or should be, all about hitting. Coach: do you want to comment on that?"

"Yes, I do," Kirby said. "First, I want to commend Patrick for agreeing to appear before this intimidating Board of grown-ups, and to clarify that he didn't do anything wrong."

"I agree," Crotz said.

"Second," Coach said, "I disagree that the pitcher is supposed to throw the ball so the hitter can hit it. That's not the way the game is played at the professional level. Pro pitchers try to get batters out."

Three of the opposing team's dads rose to their feet, and all were muttering about this last comment.

"Please be seated," Crotz said, "We know your position." The dads reluctantly sat down.

Crotz spoke again. "Patrick, could you come up here, please." Patrick looked at his coach. Coach Kirby motioned for him to approach the Board's table.

When Patrick was standing directly in front of the long line of directors, Crotz asked him: "Do you practice throwing?" Crotz already knew the answer to the question. He had sent Feller to the Wall.

Patrick looked Crotz in the eye, and said: "Yes. I have been throwing baseballs at a target I chalked on a wall for about a year."

"How many times?" a Board member asked.

"Fifty balls each time, almost every day." Patrick said. All eight directors were impressed at that.

"Did you hold every pitch you threw in the first game the same?" Crotz asked.

"No," Patrick replied. "A man came by one day and showed me how to hold pitches differently."

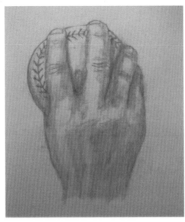

"Who was the man?" Crotz asked, although he knew the answer.

"He told me his name was Bob Feller," Patrick said.

"The Bob Feller?" Crotz asked, feigning surprise.

"Yes," Patrick said.

"Can you show me how you held the ball in the first game?" Crotz asked, producing a baseball. Patrick did not take the ball offered. Instead, he took one from his jacket pocket.

"I carry this with me," Patrick said.

Then he continued. "I throw my straight fastball by holding it near my fingertips and with my fingers across the seams, like this." He held up the ball with his fingers extending across the seams.

"I call it my four seam fastball because the baseball has four seams,"

Patrick said. "It goes pretty straight."

"Did you throw any other pitches?" Grayce Crotz asked.

"Yes," said Patrick. "I held my other fast ball with my fingers along one seam, pointed toward the horseshoe in the seams." He showed them the hold. His index finger was up against one seam.

"When I hold my fastball that way, it tails a little at the end, toward a right-handed hitter," Patrick said. "Mr. Feller showed me that."

"Did you throw any other pitches?" George Bebble asked.

"Yes. I threw a curveball at the first game," Patrick said. "I held it like this, with my fingers between the seams," he said, showing them. "When I throw it, I turn my wrist," he said, flicking his wrist. Patrick's middle finger was up against the seam on the right.

"Did Feller show you that?" Mr. Crotz asked.

"No," Patrick said. "I was talking to a tennis player one day, and she said she twisted her racquet sometimes to put spin on the ball. I thought to myself that maybe I could do that with a baseball. It took me a while, but I can now hit the target with my Curve."

Because Board members asked only what pitches he had thrown in the first game, Patrick did not feel compelled to discuss his Change. He had not thrown it.

"Very impressive," Crotz said. The Board is going to discuss this among ourselves. We will be right back." With that, the eight directors adjourned to a room behind their table.

They returned in about five minutes. Crotz spoke: "This game is about more than just hitting. My notes indicate it is also about pitching, fielding, base running, coaching, team play, and a lot more."

He went on: "Patrick, you are an exceptional player. We have concluded that you should continue to pitch as best you can. We considered the recommendation of these dads to move you up to the next level, to pitch against older players. The Board unanimously rejects that idea."

"That's not fair," the loudest dad of an opposing player said. The other dads murmured their agreement with him.

"It is fair," Crotz quickly said. "We will not penalize a player for working hard and doing his best. Patrick has worked hard at pitching."

Crotz went on: "I also note that he braved coming before us today. We would have understood if he had declined to come. Because he was here, we learned that he is not only skillful, but also honest, and resourceful. It would reflect badly on us to penalize him for that."

"Then move him up," one of the dads said.

"No." Crotz said emphatically. "It is in the interest of your sons to bat against him."

The dads were too shocked at that to respond. Their quizzical looks seemed to cry out: "How can that be?"

"The reason I say that," Crotz continued, "is that hitting against Patrick will level up your sons. He will force them to become better hitters. And we are not going to take away a chance for your sons to become better players. In addition, we urge you to follow Patrick's work ethic. Pitch to your sons and help them practice hitting."

The dads said nothing.

"One more thing." Crotz said. "This Board will never again convene to consider parent complaints. Our mission is to spread Little League to every state, and the world. We will work toward that."

He then turned to Patrick, and said, "Patrick, good luck in your next game."

"Thank you," Patrick said. He noticed the Little League logo embroidered in a cloth hanging down from the table. Even as Crotz gathered it up, Patrick caught sight of the three words on it: "Character. Courage. Loyalty."

As they left, Coach Kirby said loudly for the departing dads to hear: "Well done, Patrick."

CHAPTER 5

To give Patrick a break, Tommy also pitched games. He was as good a pitcher as he was a shortstop. He had a strong arm and a good fastball. It allowed Patrick to continue his practice throwing. He had to rest his arm a few days after each game. When Patrick was not pitching, he played right field. In other games, he sat out, letting Charlie play. For Patrick, that was fine. It was all about the team.

Behind Patrick's and Tommy's pitching, the Red Sox were in first place, well ahead of their competition.

One evening, Patrick was pitching to Robby. Tommy was at shortstop, fielding ground balls. Coach Kirby was hitting grounders to them and flies to the outfield. They practiced in the evening because Saturdays were game days and Coach worked at Bethlehem Steel during the day.

"Alright, let's go home," Coach Kirby yelled. The players started picking up their gear. Coach started walking to his car.

A girl who had been watching the practice came over to Tommy, kissed him on the cheek, and said: "Ice cream!" She turned and headed for the ice cream parlor.

First baseman John "Jack" Losch" started walking toward Tommy, who was almost to the first base line. John, a grin on his face, stepped in front of Tommy, and broke into a mocking, sing song: "Tommy's got a girlfriend! Tommy's got a girlfriend!"

Tommy never thought about it. It happened instinctively. He punched Jack in the stomach.

Jack doubled over in pain. Patrick, who saw it, didn't like what "Big John" had said, but he was appalled at what Tommy had just done to a teammate.

Coach Kirby saw it too. He had looked back when John started his sing song mockery, and witnessed the punch. He came back, walked up to Tommy, and said: "Tommy, you're benched. You can practice, but no games for you."

Sure enough. The next Saturday, Tommy sat on the bench. Patrick walked a batter in the first inning, something he rarely did. The new boy at shortstop let two consecutive grounders go through his legs. The next batter hit a high line drive at the shortstop. Tommy would have jumped and caught it. It went over the new boy's head into left field. Two runs scored.

Patrick pitched a good game, but his team seemed down-hearted. They couldn't hit. They lost 3-0.

Jiménez pitched the next game. Patrick thought as he watched him: "That's not pitching." Jimmy's problem was that he was a born center fielder. He was used to throwing the ball high and letting it come down to his infield cut-off. His pitches were almost always high. No matter how many times Robby would come out and tell him: "Keep it down," it was always the same. Jimmy walked in four runs in the first five innings he threw. The left fielder who relieved him did little better. The Red Sox lost 10-4.

The next game was more of the same. Patrick pitched his heart out. When the new shortstop made two more errors, Coach Kirby moved him to second base. He moved his steady second baseman, Kyle, to shortstop. Kyle did well, all things considered. But that didn't help what was happening at second base. More errors. Patrick pitched a three-hitter, but the Midgets lost, 5-4. They were now out of first place by one game.

The next two games went the same way.

Patrick's mind was racing. He watched as Tommy got up from the bench, having sat out yet another game. Patrick understood Coach disciplining Tommy. Tommy never should have hit Jack. But Patrick couldn't help thinking of the team: this was killing their team and its chances to come in first.

As Coach Kirby neared his car, Patrick broke into a dead run. He caught Coach Kirby just before he drove off.

"Coach, can I talk to you?" Kirby rolled down his window.

"Sure. What do you want?"

"Uh, well, I was just wondering..." Patrick was mad at himself. He had rehearsed this in his mind for several days, and

now he had trouble finding words.

"Ah, well, Coach, our team is losing. Our team isn't the same without Tommy. Uh, I was wondering, um, if Tommy apologized to Jack, could Tommy could play again?"

There. He said it. He stared at Coach expectantly.

Coach Kirby narrowed his eyes. He was prepared for this request, just not from Patrick.

"I've been waiting for Tommy to suggest that," Coach said. "But yes, if he does, he can play." Patrick's eyes widened.

"Coach, can you wait?" Patrick asked, as he bolted toward the field. He tracked down Tommy, and confronted him.

"You need to come with me," Patrick said. He turned and started running, only to stop and turn back, and yell: "Come on!" The two were running toward Coach's car together, with Patrick talking most of the way. They stopped in front of Coach, who was out of his car. The three stared at each other in silence.

Finally, Patrick shot Tommy a look and asked: "Well?"

"Coach," said Tommy, looking down at the ground, "if I apologize to Jack, can I play?"

Coach Kirby replied, "Yes, but you have to do it in front of the whole team." With that, Coach started walking toward the field. Patrick and Tommy were close behind.

Coach neared the mound, and yelled: "Circle."

The entire team had been watching this unfold. They quickly sat cross-legged in a circle around Coach Kirby.

"John, come here." Big John got up and walked toward Coach.

"Tommy, you're at bat," Coach said.

Tommy got up and stood in front of Jack. Jack thought back to the last time they were this close. Tommy spoke: "Jack, I'm sorry I hit you. I apologize." Jack responded: "I'm sorry for what I said."

Coach then said softly: "Tommy, you're at short next Saturday." The team erupted. Patrick was close to laughing he was so happy.

***

The team started winning again with Tommy at shortstop and relieving Patrick. At the last practice, Patrick asked if he could pitch the next game. Coach Kirby said, "No. You pitched the last game."

"Coach," let me do this," Patrick said. He didn't mention the ice bag his mother invented to put on his sore arm at night. "We're tied for first place. Let me pitch this last game. You can take me out if I get hit." He didn't say: "If I get sore." he said: "If I get hit." Patrick's one thought was about the team.

Coach said very slowly: "OK. I shouldn't do this. Just this one time." Coach wanted to win the next game as badly as Patrick. But he didn't want to hurt him.

"Thanks!" Patrick said emphatically. He was about to pitch the biggest game of his life.

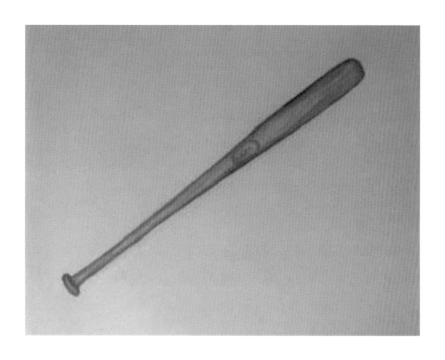

CHAPTER 6

Patrick struck out the first two batters in the final and deciding game of the regular season. And then the train went off the rails.

It started with a routine infield grounder. The second baseman's throw to first was in the dirt and got past Jack. A shallow single to left center brought him home from second base. Patrick walked the next batter as his curveball refused to behave. A long triple to left center scored two runs and left a runner in scoring position. Thankfully, Patrick struck out the next batter.

"Woohoo" came from the third base line.

The Red Sox needed runs. Instead, they went three up and three down. They were on the field again.

This Lycoming Dairy team had some big boys on it. The first batter Patrick faced in the second inning was the biggest. Patrick was wracking his brain to come up with an edge—any edge—against this batter. Then he remembered something Bob Feller had told him: "Watch how they hold the bat."

He noticed that the batter held his hands high and the bat straight up in the air. Patrick called time out to talk with Robby.

"This guy wants a low pitch to golf out of the park. I'm going to pitch him high."

"OK," Robby said, and assumed his crouch behind the plate.

Just as he had practiced, Patrick threw for the top half of his chalked target, which corresponded roughly to the strike zone.

"Strike one!" the umpire yelled, as the batter let the pitch go.

Patrick followed it with a cut fastball in the same place. The batter didn't like it any better.

"Strike two!" the umpire called.

Patrick knew the batter would be swinging. He threw a pitch that started on a line toward the middle of the plate, but at the last second, curved down and away from the batter. Thinking it was the pitch he wanted, the batter swung over it.

"Strike three! You're out!"

The next batter held his bat differently. He held it straight back over his shoulder. Patrick told Robby how he would pitch him.

The first pitch curved down and away and the batter let it go.

"Strike one!" the umpire called.

Patrick followed it with a straight fastball down at the batter's knees. He let it go. To hit a low pitch, he had to lift his bat and drop it down on the ball. There was no time with Patrick's fastball. A curveball struck the batter out. The next batter hit a grounder to Tommy at short, and his laser beam to first base ended the inning.

"Woohoo!" came a shout from the left field line.

The first two Red Sox, Tommy and Jack, hit back-to-back singles. Patrick came to bat. He knew the gravity of the situation. They needed runs. As he faced the pitcher, he repeated his favorite saying to himself when he was at bat: "See the bat hit the ball." It was impossible to do that without watching the ball all the way to the bat. He hit a first-pitch single into right field. Tommy scored easily. They scored four runs that inning, as the Red Sox' bats came to life.

The next inning, Patrick not only watched how the batters held their bats, but also where they stood in relation to the plate. The first batter crowded the plate. Patrick pitched him on the inside half of the plate. Twice the batter backed away from inside strikes. The batter then backed off the plate slightly, and Patrick threw his Curve. It went down and away. The batter swung over it.

Robby was now all over where the batters stood and how they held their bats. He called pitches accordingly. The next three innings Lycoming Dairy blanked.

Meanwhile, the Red Sox piled on the runs. For the final inning, Coach Kirby told Patrick he wanted him to play right field and let Tommy close out the game.

"Coach," Patrick responded, "I can do this. It's best for the team for Tommy to stay at short."

Coach Kirby looked at Patrick, knew he was right, but wasn't sure he should let Patrick continue.

"How does your arm feel?" he asked Patrick.

"Fine," Patrick responded.

"Alright, but if you start throwing balls, I'm putting Tommy in."

Instead of leading with his fastball, Patrick started the first batter with his Curve. Strike one. Instead of following it up with a fastball, he threw a second Curve. Strike two. Not having any idea what would follow, the batter flailed at the four seam fastball that seemed faster than any he had seen.

"Strike three!" the umpire yelled.

Patrick pitched the next batter the same. The batter was not ready for any of the pitches and the umpire called him out on strikes.

Then Robby called for a fastball on the first pitch. It seemed like a good idea. The batter, a big older boy, hit the ball deep into center. Jimmy took off after it at full speed. He caught it running away from the plate. Unfortunately, he was right at the fence. He hit the wooden fence at full speed, bouncing off the boards to the ground. He wasn't big enough to break the boards.

He rose slowly, and showed the umpire the ball in his glove. "You're out!" called the umpire, sealing the win.

"Woohoo! Woohoo! Woohoo!"

Before Patrick could turn and wave to Wanda, a mass of young boys buried him under a pile of bodies. Jimmy got there late and jumped on to celebrate winning the season. Coach Kirby came running out and dug out Patrick from under the mass of bodies.

"Are you OK?" the Coach asked his winning pitcher.

"I'm great," said Patrick, and proceeded to shake hands and back slap his teammates. It was the greatest moment of his young life.

The first Little League series ever to be played, the National Little League Tournament, would start in eight days.

***

Five days later, Coach Kirby came to Patrick's home to talk to Patrick. They sat at the kitchen table.

"Patrick, I've come because I have some news about the upcoming National Little League Tournament," Coach said. Patrick was excited. This was the news he had been waiting for.

"We are in the Maynard League," Coach said. "Coach Charlie Scudder will coach the Maynard League Midgets in the National Tournament. He has already picked his team of fourteen players."

Coach narrowed his eyes as he looked at Patrick. "Coach Scudder is picking hitters and concentrating on older kids. He asked me to tell you he did not select you for the Tournament games. He knows of your pitching, but he wants hitters." Coach went on: "He told me, I don't care how many runs the other team scores. We'll score more."

Patrick fought back tears. He said simply: "OK."

Coach Kirby turned and left. He knew there was nothing he could say that would make this easier on Patrick. Patrick talked to his mother for a long time. Then he went to his room to be alone.

It was the worst day of Patrick's life.

CHAPTER 7

The next day, Patrick walked to the Wall. He had two used baseballs. He threw mostly fastballs. Anger and frustration drove their speed and ferocity. Patrick was sure his arm would fly off as he smashed the balls against the Wall.

The seams on one of the balls split apart after twenty-five throws. It was used when he started, and Patrick was not surprised that it came apart. The seams on the other ball gave way at forty throws. He examined the loose covers, realized the balls were unusable, and headed home.

It was the first time ever he had not thrown all fifty pitches. It no longer seemed to matter.

At home, he saw a strange car parked in front of the house. He stepped inside. A man at the table was talking to his mother.

"Patrick," his mother said. "This is Mr. Scudder." Charles Scudder stood up and shook Patrick's hand.

"Please sit down," he said. "I have some things I want to discuss with you."

Patrick nodded, but said nothing. He thought to himself: "Here comes his reason for not picking me."

Coach Scudder started talking. "Coach Kirby told you I did not select you as one of my fourteen players for the Maynard League's National Tournament team. I'm sorry for that, but I was looking for older boys and hitters."

"I know," Patrick said softly. He forced himself to look Scudder in the eye. Coach Scudder went on: "Well, one of my boys is sick, very sick. The doctor says he can't play. The games start in two days. I am up against it. I'm asking you to take his place. Would you do that?"

Patrick's eyes lit up. He straightened up and said: "Yes! Wow! I can't believe it!"

Coach Scudder said: "Well, I thought that might be your answer, but, I'm still relieved to hear it."

"One more thing," Scudder said. "They have already printed the rosters for the National Tournament. Your name does not appear anywhere for the Maynard League Midgets. I'm sorry. I can take care of introducing you to the umpires and getting you into games, if I need you. But they won't re-do the printed rosters. Your name may not appear anywhere."

Coach Scudder looked intently at Patrick while talking, hoping for a positive answer. Patrick absorbed the news, collected his thoughts, and said; "That doesn't matter to me. It's all about the team. I want to help the team."

Coach Scudder responded: "Thank you. Coach Kirby told me you would be a great teammate. We practice tonight at the field. We get it for an hour and a half, starting at six. You will throw to Bill Gallagher. See you there."

He stood up, shook hands with Patrick and his mother, and turned to Patrick: "One more question," Scudder said. "Can you hit?"

Patrick nodded and said: "I hit three doubles, a triple, and a bunch of singles. I watch the ball to the bat."

"So glad to hear that," Scudder said, and left.

Patrick looked at his mother. He had a tear in one eye. She hugged him and said: "Patrick, we are so proud of you. I cannot wait to tell your father. He will want to take off work to watch the games."

Patrick said: 'I guess it's lucky I didn't get my full practice in today."

***

When Patrick got to the field that evening, he introduced himself to catcher Bill Gallagher.

"I've been expecting you," Gallagher said. "Coach talks to us first, and then we practice."

The players gathered around Coach Scudder. Patrick almost sat down, but noticed that the other players were standing. Coach

Scudder was a man of few words.

"Practice like you mean it. The Tournament starts in two days. We have a new player on the team. Meet Patrick. He says he can hit. We are glad he joined the team. Let's go!"

The players took their positions. Patrick started throwing to Gallagher. He threw his fastball, cut fastball, and Curve. He saved the Change for later.

Coach Scudder hit fly balls and grounders to his fielders. When they were finished, Patrick climbed on his bike and headed home.

Gallagher walked over to Coach Scudder, who was headed home to get some sleep. The coach worked the third shift at Bethlehem Steel and was dog tired.

"This Patrick is really something," Gallagher said. "I'm glad we got him."

CHAPTER 8

It was the Monday before the games started. All the players' eyes were on Coach Scudder.

"This is the first National Little League Tournament. We should really call it "The Pennsylvania Tournament" because all but one of the twelve teams come from Pennsylvania. We play Jersey Shore in our first game Wednesday. You can all be proud you are playing in this Tournament. But for me, I don't just want to play in it, I want to win it all. Do you?"

The players shouted: "Yeah! Win it all!"

"All right then," he went on. "Practice like you mean it. Batters, get hits. Fielders, get your body in front of the ball. Pitchers, pitch ahead—stay ahead. Let's go."

This was their last practice before the start of the Tournament on Tuesday. Patrick was hitting all his spots. Wherever Gallagher put his glove, Patrick hit it. He was on. Coach Scudder stood behind Patrick for a while. He liked what he saw.

"Good job, Patrick," Coach Scudder told him after practice. "Give your arm a rest and be ready for Wednesday."

On Tuesday, Patrick and the rest of the team watched as Original League annihilated Sunday School League 15-0. In Game 2, Lincoln League beat Montoursville, Pennsylvania 7-2. Lincoln League and Montoursville were out. It rained on Tuesday, and two additional games would be crammed into Wednesday.

In the third game, Brandon League took out Montgomery, Pennsylvania 14-2. Now the fourth game finally came: the Maynard Midgets would play the team from Jersey Shore, Pennsylvania.

The Midgets carried a big lead into the seventh inning, and Patrick closed the game out with two strikeouts and an infield groundout.

"Woohoo," came from the third base line, where Patrick's mother sat with her arm around Wanda and Patrick's father looked on proudly. On to game two!

Maynard League drew the power house Brandon League in their second game. Brandon League had embarrassed the Montgomery, Pennsylvania team in their first game, and came in talking about going all the way.

Coach Scudder was worried. He needed strong pitching and his hitters had to show up.

They did.

The Midgets dispatched Brandon 10-4. Patrick once again sealed the game with a combination of fastballs and curveballs that Brandon couldn't handle.

"Woohoo," came from the third baseline, and the Midgets headed for game three.

Game three didn't go as intended. Coach Scudder's hitters didn't show up.

The Lincoln League team came to play. Seven hard-fought innings led to a tie, and the game went into extra innings. The Midget's pitcher threw seven strong innings. But in extra innings in the eighth, he walked two batters, hit the third, and got no outs.

Coach Scudder headed to the mound. He took the ball from the pitcher, and called for Patrick, who had watched the game from the bench.

At Coach's signal, he had thrown a few warm-up pitches while this disaster unfolded.

When he arrived at the mound, Coach Scudder handed him the ball, and said: "Patrick, this game is now all about pitching. We get last bats, but you have to hold them. Do the team proud."

Gallagher was standing there as well. "Pitch this guy high," he said. Patrick saw the batter holding his bat straight up in the air.

"Got it," Patrick said. Patrick could not see his mother and Wanda with their faces in their hands, or hear his father saying how unfair it was to put Patrick in with no outs and the bases loaded.

Gallagher crouched behind the plate. Patrick went into a full wind-up. He stepped forward and threw a high strike on the inside of the plate. The batter let it go.

"Strike one," the umpire called. "Pitch ahead—stay ahead" rang in Patrick's ears. The batter stepped back a little from the plate, anticipating another inside fastball.

For some reason, Patrick threw two balls in a row. Gallagher called for a curveball. It went wide of the plate. Patrick went back to the fastball. The batter swung, but could not catch up to it.

"Strike two!" the umpire yelled. Full count. Another ball would give Brandon the lead. The crowd, both benches, and the fielders, went silent. The next pitch had to be a strike. Gallagher called for another fastball. The batter swung and hit it—hard.

Right at Patrick. It hit him in the stomach—at ninety miles an hour.

Patrick fell to his knees. It was every pitcher's nightmare. But he had no time to think about the pain, worry about getting his breath, or the crowd's reaction. The runner on third was streaking home.

Patrick picked up the ball in front of him, and still on his knees, rifled a throw to Gallagher. With his foot on the plate, Gallagher caught the ball a half-second ahead of the runner.

"Out!" the umpire called.

"Woohoo!"

Patrick was still on his knees, but the crowd was on their feet. The next thing Patrick knew, Coach Scudder was crouching down, looking him in the eye.

"Gutsy play. Thanks for making the out. Give me the ball."

Patrick stood up. It hurt to stand.

"No!" Patrick said. "Please give me a chance. If I walk a batter or get hit, you can take me out."

Patrick's mother and father were on Coach's side. They wanted Coach to relieve their son and get him out of harm's way.

Coach Scudder thought long and hard. The umpire came up and asked what was going on.

"He's staying in," Coach said. "He just needs to catch his breath." With that, Coach went back to the bench and the umpire behind the plate. Patrick was right. Why argue with success?

Gallagher came out to the mound. "Let's not start with the fastball," the catcher said. "Curve and then the fastball."

As Gallagher went back behind the plate, Patrick stared at

the older boy at the plate.

It was Gregory.

The last time Patrick had faced him, he had hit Gregory in the stomach and chest. Today, Patrick wanted to put him away differently.

"You can hit 'im, Greg," came a shout from his dad in the stands. Patrick ignored it.

Patrick's Curve started toward the right-handed Gregory, who was crowding the plate and expecting a first-pitch fastball. The last batter told him to watch for it. Gregory stepped out of the way, as the curveball bent over the inside of the plate.

"Strike one."

For some reason, Patrick followed the strike with two balls in a row. Gallagher came to the mound. "You're steering it," he said. "Just let it fly. Give me your cut fastball. See the glove, hit the glove."

Patrick let his cut fastball fly, without trying to steer it, and got the second strike. Gregory watched it go by, unnerved a little by the late movement on the pitch, as it tailed in.

Gregory was holding his bat straight up in the air. Gallagher called for a high strike. Patrick tried, but the pitch went too high.

"Ball three!" called the ump. Full count. One pitch away from walking in a run. Gregory smiled at Patrick.

Gallagher called for another cut fastball. But Patrick had a different idea. He held his right hand in his glove so the batter could not see him grip the ball. Patrick wound up, and, with a prayer, let it fly.

Gregory expected a fastball. He started swinging, tried to slow his swing, and then stop it altogether. He awkwardly went down on one knee, almost falling over as the slow pitch went by him.

"Strike three!" called the ump. Gregory walked away with his head down.

Gallagher came running out to the mound.

"WHAT WAS THAT?" he asked in a loud voice. "That's my Change," Patrick said matter-of-factly. "I wasn't going to use it because it's hard to control."

"I didn't know you had a change-up," Gallagher said. "That pitch is a lot slower than your fastball. Let's use it as an out pitch."

Patrick understood. Get two strikes and use the Change for the out.

He noticed that the next right-handed batter held his bat at a slight angle off his shoulder. He was neither too close or far from the plate. Gallagher called for a fastball.

Patrick hit his spot. Right down the middle of the plate, waist high. But it was too good. The batter swung and hit the ball—hard.

The ball went high into left field, right along the line. It was hit deep. The Midget's left fielder, Louis "Scrap Iron" Baity, chased it. He had been playing a little shallow, and this ball was over his head. He ran facing the fence at full speed. Patrick thought: "Grand slam."

But Scrap Iron was no ordinary fielder. Running flat out, he closed fast. Running away from the plate, he caught the ball over his shoulder, with his glove outstretched in front of him.

Before anyone could react to this spectacular catch, Scrap Iron hit the wooden fence at full speed. He dislodged three boards in it, and lay on top of them. Ignoring the pain, he got to his feet, and showed the umpire the ball in his glove.

"That's an out!" the umpire yelled.

"Woohoo!" The spectators, including Patrick's family, and Wanda, erupted in applause.

Scrap Iron's hat had fallen off. As the team left the field, Patrick remained on the mound. His African American teammate put his hat back on, off to one side. Patrick's hand went for his hat.

But he did not just tip his hat to Scrap Iron, so-called because, by reputation, he was tough as iron. Patrick removed his hat and held it over his heart. Scrap Iron saluted him as he started to run for the bench. He was limping.

When Baity got to the mound, Patrick put his hand on the outfielder's shoulder and they walked to the bench together. Scrap Iron was no longer limping.

The Midgets scored the winning run in the eighth inning. The papers didn't know Patrick's name and attributed his pitching to another player. Patrick didn't care.

At the end of the game, Patrick approached Gregory. "Good game," Patrick said, extending his hand. "Thanks," a surprised Gregory replied, as they shook hands. Carl Crotz smiled approvingly as he witnessed "Little League Character" on full display.

Then Patrick went with his family and Wanda for ice cream, and had three scoops of chocolate.

"You used your Change," Wanda noted proudly.

"I did," Patrick said.

"Who was that big guy you struck out?" his father asked.

"That was Gregory," Patrick said. His father smiled. Patrick's mother had told him about the tomatoes.

The Maynard Midgets had made the final game of the first National Little League Tournament.

CHAPTER 9

The first game had been on Tuesday. Now it was Friday. In addition to the grueling schedule, the 90 degree heat took a toll.

But as the time for the final game of the first National Little League Tournament neared, none of that mattered. Players were excited. 2,500 spectators lined the field, thanks in part to sympathetic employers like Bethlehem Steel, which let Patrick's father, and others, take off from work for the game. Most sat or stood on the levee between the field and the West Branch Susquehanna River.

The Lock Haven All Stars had beaten the New Jersey team 5-1 to earn the right to face the Maynard League Midgets. The All Stars were from Pennsylvania, but not Williamsport. Of the six Williamsport teams in the National Tournament, only the Midgets made it to the final game.

The first National Little League Tournament was "National" in name only. The New Jersey team that the All Stars had eliminated was the only team in the Tournament from outside of Pennsylvania. Carl Stotz and the Board, however, considered even that a victory. Through their efforts, Little League had spread beyond the state of Pennsylvania.

That Friday evening, excitement reigned. Patrick and the other Midgets knew the All Stars would be tough, but he and his team were ready. Excitement would not prevent giving it their best.

Patrick secretly wished his team was not called the "Midgets." He was tall for his age, and wondered why they didn't have a better sounding name. After all, the other league named Lock Haven the "All Stars." If it had been up to Patrick, he would have called his team the "Yankees."

At game time, Coach Scudder called them together and said: "I'm proud of all you, win or lose. But I have to tell you—you will like winning better than losing. So don't stop now. Give it everything you have. Let's go!"

The All Stars batted first and went three up and three down. Then the Midgets took over. From the start, they were on fire.

First, they were patient and drew walks. When Russell, the All Stars pitcher, started putting pitches over the plate, the Midgets started hitting them all over the field. By the second inning, they had seven runs.

The game was lopsided from then on. Excitement for the Midgets and their fans started to mount as they poured on more runs. Lock Haven's early errors didn't help it any. This was a level where mistakes proved costly.

The All Stars coach changed pitchers in the third inning, but it didn't help. The Midgets scored five more runs and seemed unstoppable. Don Stover hit two home runs, as did Ed Ungard. Tony Ingersol, the Midgets' third baseman, went four for four, batting 1,000 for the day. Scudder's bats were in full swing.

When the last inning rolled around, Coach Scudder used Patrick to seal the game. Gallagher had Patrick throwing early fastballs to speed up the All Stars' bats, followed by the Curve or the Change that got their bats out ahead of the pitch. The All Stars went two up and two down in the seventh inning, both strikeouts.

"Woohoo! Woohoo!"

All of the Midgets and their fans were standing. The next All Star was a big kid with a bat held straight up on the air.

Patrick threw a high fastball on the inside half of the plate.

"Strike one!" the umpire called.

The batter backed up a little. Patrick's curveball started toward the middle of the plate, but broke sharply down and away. The batter swung over it.

It was not lost on anyone that the Midgets were one pitch away from the biggest win of their young lives. Gallagher called for the Change.

Patrick delivered it just like his fastball, the way he had practiced it. The batter was ready for a fastball, and started swinging early. In desperation, he tried unsuccessfully to slow his swing, and then stop it. He did neither.

"Strike three!" the umpire yelled. The Midgets won 16-7.

"Woohoo!"

The Midget's bench erupted. The fielders came running in and converged on the mound. Slaps on the back followed for five minutes, as the Williamsport fans screamed in delight. Under Coach's orders, they did not bury the pitcher on the mound.

Carl Stotz looked on with a broad smile. Every team was his team, but he couldn't hide his satisfaction that a Williamsport team had won the first National Little League Tournament.

Coach Kirby came to the bench and congratulated Coach Scudder.

"Thanks for Patrick," Scudder said. "We wouldn't have made it here without him." They talked further while the celebration on the mound went on.

The 2,500 fans dispersed slowly. Many were Williamsport residents, and they couldn't get enough of their new young heroes. It was a good feeling for everyone.

For the Midgets players, every win had been better than the preceding one. But this one was by far the best.

For Patrick, it was the best day of his life.

CHAPTER 10

Amid the sea of spectators flowing onto the field, Patrick saw his parents and Wanda along the third baseline. He waved to them.

Gradually the crowd dispersed. The team started to drift away from the mound. Patrick was still taking it all in. He didn't want the moment to end.

Gallagher called to him from the first base line.

"Patrick. Come here. Pictures." Sure enough, the team was assembling for a team picture.

Just as Patrick was about to join them, he heard someone say: "Patrick. Can I talk to you?" It was a man in a suit. Bob Feller was approaching from the third base side.

"Yes, sir." Patrick answered.

"You did well in the Tournament," Feller said. "Can you wait a minute?"

"Sure," Patrick said. Feller walked over to the Midgets' bench and picked up a ball. The game ball was nowhere to be seen. Coach Scudder probably had it.

"Thanks for waiting," Feller said.

"Bob, we have to go," Feller's wife insisted from the sidelines.

"Just a minute dear," Feller said.

While Patrick waited, Feller was writing on the ball. While he wrote, he said: "I noticed how you used the pitches I showed you. You were also reading bats. And I saw you take that ball in the stomach and stay in there. That was pretty gutsy."

"Thanks," Patrick said.

He gave the ball to Patrick, who read the writing aloud:
Honest Brave Resourceful
Robert Bullet Bob Feller

"That is really nice of you," Patrick said, almost in disbelief.

"You earned it," Feller said. "I want to support Little League. It's a great idea. I hope it catches on."

"One more thing," Feller said. "I was impressed that you didn't ask me for my autograph the first time we met."

"Thank you!" Patrick said, taking his eyes off the ball to look Feller in the eye.

"You're welcome," Feller said, as he and his wife headed for their car. He had an appointment of his own on the mound for the Cleveland Indians the next day.

Gallagher came running up as Patrick stared at the ball.

"You missed the team picture!" his catcher said.

Patrick handed him the ball. Gallagher inspected it.

"That was Bob Feller?" he asked incredulously.

"Yup," Patrick said. "He showed me some pitches a while ago."

"Wow," Gallagher said. The team picture seemed far less important at the moment.

Patrick said good-bye to his teammates, showing them the signed baseball. Coach Scudder confessed that he knew Feller was there, and had singled out Patrick as a favorite.

Patrick joined his parents and Wanda for the ride home. They were impressed with the signed baseball from Feller. Patrick's father told Patrick that Feller had introduced himself to them before the game.

When they dropped Wanda off at her house, she kissed Patrick on the cheek. She quickly told him that his mother had given her permission to do that. Patrick smiled. It was OK.

On the way home, his father picked up a clear glass case with a wooden base under it. The ball fit in it, and Patrick's father carefully put the ball and case on the mantle. It stood there by itself, telling the story of the Maynard Midgets and Bob Feller.

That night, Patrick went to sleep dreaming of winning more big games—and hitting his spot five times.

1947 National Little League Tournament
Maynard League Midgets

Every Little Leaguer's Dream

Signing letter of Jonathan Metzger, the author's son,
with the Kansas City Royals, with his
baseball card and Royals Logo

Every Little Leaguer's Dream

EPILOGUE

In 1948, the Lock Haven All Stars win the National Little League Tournament. Little League grows to 94 leagues around the country. Lock Haven beats a league that year from St. Petersburg, Florida. The National Little League Tournament is later renamed the Little League World Series. In either 1950 or 1951, (historians cannot agree), Kathryn "Kay" Johnston-Massar becomes the first girl to play Little League baseball. Her mother cuts her braids and dresses her like a boy. She calls herself "Tubby" because of her love for Little Lulu comic books. She earns her way onto the team and plays first base. When she tells her coach she is a girl, he says: "That's OK. You're a darned good player." Her teammates call her Tubby, even after they learn her secret. She plays only one season. The next year a new rule takes place. The "Tubby Rule" states that "Girls are not eligible under any circumstances." The rule is changed in 1974 when girls are allowed to play. As a result of the rule change, Mo'ne Davis, a 13-year-old African American girl, pitches two shutouts in the 2014 Little League World Series—one in the regionals, and one in the semi-finals in Williamsport. She makes the cover of Sports Illustrated, and appears on late-night television shows. (Washington Post, August 15, 2019, C8.). In 1953, the first Little League game is played on television. The first international champion comes from Monterey, Mexico, in 1957. By 2014, there are over 7,000 chartered Little Leagues worldwide. There are Little Leagues in Kyrgyzstan, the Middle East, Japan, Taiwan, many other countries, and on the continents of Australia and Africa.

Carl Stotz' vision of expanding Little League far and wide is fulfilled.

Credits

Picture of Original Field, courtesy of Wikipedia.

Other Historical Little League information, courtesy of the Little League Museum website.

Use of the term Little League, and the Little League Logo courtesy of Little League Baseball®, Incorporated, a non-profit membership organization.

Results of National Little League Tournament of 1947, courtesy of Wikipedia.

Description of final game of the National Little League Tournament of 1947, courtesy of Lock Haven Express newspaper article, August 25, 1947.

THE END